A Kalmus Classic E

Jean Louis
DUPORT

TWENTY-ONE ETUDES

FOR CELLO

K 02066

Kalmus

JEAN-LOUIS DUPORT

The modern method of violoncello playing dates only from about the last third of the eighteenth century. While the great Italian masters had developed the art of the violin before the end of the seventeenth, it remained for the Frenchman Jean-Louis Duport to bring order and system into the method of the violoncello. His "Essay on the Art of Fingering the Violoncello and of Bowing," published about 1770, first corrected the crudities and inefficiencies of his contemporaries and predecessors in both the important elements of which it treats, and cleared the way for the development of modern technique. Duport was the son of a ballet master, and was born in Paris in 1749. He first devoted himse to the violin; but the success of his elder brothe Jean-Pierre as a 'cellist stimulated him to emulation. He became his pupil, and soon surpassed him in skill. He made his début at the Concerts Spirituels in Paris in 1768, the same year in which the gifted Boccherini appeared there; and was famous as a performer before his twentieth year. In 1782 Viotti came to Paris, and the profound impression that he made with his disclosure of an art riper, fuller, and more developed in every way than anything that had before been known in the French capital, was general. It had a marked influence on the young 'cellist, who determined to achieve, on his own instrument, something of the same breadth of style, beauty of tone, elegance and brilliancy. He set to work to accomplish this, and contemporary testimony is abundant as to his success.

In 1789 the outbreak of the French Revolution drove the Duport Brothers out of France, and they betook themselves to Berlin, where they obtained positions in the Royal band. Jean-Louis was received as the first violoncellist of his time, and for seventeen years he maintained that position there. The confusion and disaster of the Napoleonic war were ruinous to the musician, and he returned to Paris in 1806. His long absence had dulled the remembrance of his fame, and he had, at the age of fifty-eight, to make a new reputation for himself. He interested the public, but found all official avenues of artistic advancement closed to him. Again he had to go forth into the world to find substantial appreciation of his artistic powers. He found it first from the Spanish king, Charles IV., who was then resident at Marseilles, and who took Duport into his service. Those were uncertain times for royalty, however, and before long the movements of his royal patron again threw Duport upon his own resources. He returned to Paris, where he gave several concerts, and astonished the musical public by his youthful vigor and unimpaired technical prowess, though he was then at the age of sixty-five. Napoleon was then occupying the throne, and was ruling his empire with a lavish patronage of art. As a result of this state of affairs Duport was taken into the service of the Empress Marie-Louise, and at last into the Emperor's band, as solo violoncellist; then, into the Conservatoire as professor. It was the period of his most brilliant success, but it was not for long; for in 1819 Duport died, at the age of seventy.

He enriched the literature of his instrument with six concertos, four sonatas, duos, variations and various solo pieces, and, above all, his famous "Essay." The reforms that Duport introduced into the technique of the violoncello, set forth in this noted treatise, consist in the true fingering of the instrument, as practised ever since—that is, by semitones, only the first and second fingers being allowed to stretch a whole tone. Before his time players had attempted to finger, as upon the violin, whole tones with successive fingers. Duport also systematized the positions and adopted a methodical system of shifting. The modern way of bowing, too, owes something to Duport—the practice of an underhand grasp, as in the bow of the double bass, had not in his time been entirely given up. That these various innovations were absolutely essential to any highly developed technical skill upon the 'cello is obvious to any student of the instrument. What Duport did for it, in fact, is indicated in the remark said to have been made to him by Voltaire at Geneva: "Sir, you make me believe in miracles; you know how to turn an ox into a nightingale!"

General Explanations.

For the notation of violoncello - music three different clefs are employed, namely, the F-clef or Bass Clef  the C - clef or Tenor Clef  and the G - clef or Treble Clef

The note middle - C would be written in each of these clefs as follows:

The different strings are marked thus:

A - string.   D - string.   G - string.   C - string.

The different Positions are indicated by Pos. I, Pos. II, Pos. III, Pos. IV, etc.

A line drawn after "A - string", "D - string", etc., means that the player is to remain on that string until the end of the line.

A line drawn after "Same position" means, that all notes under this line are to be exe - cuted in the given position.

When the direction "Same position" occurs after ♀ (the sign for the thumb) it means that the thumb must remain in the same position.

♀ is the sign for the thumb.

o is the sign for the open string.

⊓ is the sign for the down-bow.

V is the sign for the up-bow.

The 4 fingers of the left hand are indicated by 1 2 3 4.

TWENTY - ONE ÉTUDES

J.L. DUPORT
(1749 - 1819)

1. Concert - Étude for independence in leading of parts, and smooth change of bow.

6

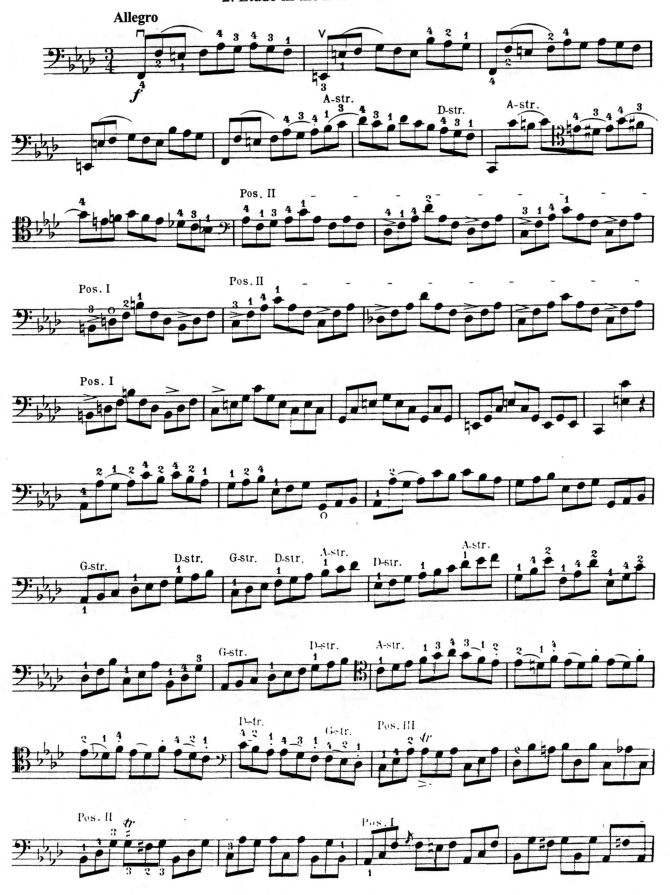

2. Étude in the middle of the bow.

3. Étude on the chromatic scale, and to strengthen the right hand.
Between nut and middle.

12

D-str.   G-str.

4. Close to the point.

Allegro moderato e marcatiss

16

5. Middle of bow.

18

6.* With springing bow, between middle and nut.

Allegro

* This Étude is by Berteau.

20

7. Arpeggio; long stroke; each note distinct.

Different bowing:

21

8.*) For Style. Take care that the melody is not influenced
in accentuation by the accompanying part.

Adagio cantabile

*) This Étude is by Duport the elder.

9. For different bowings and double-stops.

Allegro moderato

26

28

10.*) Springing bow, in the middle.

*) This Étude is by Duport the elder.

30

11. For springing bow. Likewise good practice at the point.

32

33

12. For various bowings.

Allegro moderato quasi andante

36

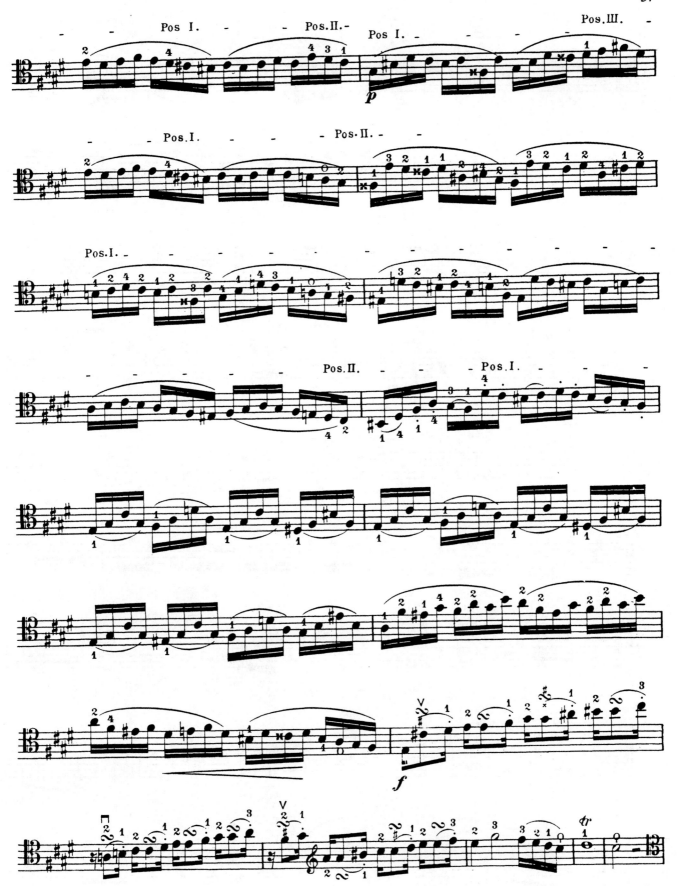

13. At the point. The staccato notes very short.

Allegro

14.

J.L. DUPORT

Andante grazioso

same Pos. same Pos.

15. Étude for the 4th finger, and in style.

47

48

16.

Adagio

17.

51

18.

Allegro maestoso

same Pos.

56

57

58

60

19. This Étude must be played throughout in the ½ Position.

Allegro

20. This Étude must be played at the point of the bow
in order that strength and lightness may be combined.

21.

65

66

68

VIOLIN

Violin Studies

DANCLA, JEAN C. (1818 - 1907)
____ (K03364) School of Mechanism,
Op. 74

DONT, JACOB (1815 - 1888)
____ (K03411) Thirty Progressive Exercises,
Op. 38

HRIMALY, JOHANN (1844 - 1915)
____ (K03554) Scale Studies

KAYSER, HEINRICH ERNST (1815 - 1888)
____ (K03575) 36 Etudes, Op. 20

KREUTZER, RODOLPHE (1766 - 1831)
____ (K03594) 42 Studies or Caprices

MAZAS, JACQUES (1782 - 1849)
____ (K03666) 75 Melodious and Progressive
Studies, Op. 36 - Vol. III

SCHRADIECK, HENRY (1849 - 1918)
____ (K03864) School of Violin
Technics

SEVCIK, OTAKAR (1852 - 1934)
____ (K03950) School of Violin Technics,
Op. 1 Vol. I - 1st Position
____ (K03951) School of Violin Technics,
Op. 1 Vol. II - 2nd to 7th
Positions
____ (K03952) School of Violin Technics,
Op. 1 Vol. III - Shifting
____ (K03957) Prep. Exercises in Double
Stopping, Op. 9

WIENIAWSKI, HENRI (1835 - 1880)
____ (K04362) Etudes-Caprices, Op. 18 -
Vol. I

WOHLFAHRT, KARL ADRIAN (1874 - 1943)
____ (K04037) 60 Studies, Op. 45 - Vol. I
(Nos. 1-30)
____ (K04038) 60 Studies, Op. 45 - Vol. II
(Nos. 31-60)

Violin Alone

BACH, JOHANN SEBASTIAN (1685 - 1750)
____ (K03024) Six Sonatas and Partitas

PAGANINI, NICCOLO (1784 - 1840)
____ (K04405) 24 Caprices, Op. 1

REGER, MAX (1873 - 1916)
____ (K09810) Two Sonatas, Op. 42
(Nos. 1 & 2)

Violin and Piano

ACCOLAY, J.B. (1845 - 1910)
____ (K03000) Three Concertinos

BACH, JOHANN SEBASTIAN (1685 - 1750)
____ (K03022) Double Concerto
____ (K03018) Six Sonatas (David) Vol. I
(Nos. 1-3)
____ (K03019) Six Sonatas (David) Vol. II
(Nos. 4-6)
____ (K03020) Violin Concerto in A minor
____ (K03021) Violin Concerto No. 2 in
E Major

BACH—Gounod
____ (K09192) Ave Maria (Meditation)

BEETHOVEN, LUDWIG van (1770 - 1827)
____ (K03150) Two Romances,
Op. 40 and 50
____ (K03140) Violin Concerto, Op. 61
(Flesch)
____ (K09269) Horn Sonata, for Horn, Violin
or Cello and Piano

BIBER, HEINRICH FRANZ (1644 - 1704)
____ (K09193) Eight Violin Sonatas

BOISDEFFRE, RENE DE (1838 - 1906)
____ (K09196) Suite Romantique, Op. 24,
Nos. 1-3

BRUCH, MAX (1838 - 1920)
____ (K03272) Violin Concerto in G
minor, Op. 26

CHAUSSON, ERNEST A. (1855 - 1899)
____ (K03290) Poeme

DVORAK, ANTONIN (1814 - 1904)
____ (K03449) Concerto in A minor, Op. 53
____ (K04375) Sonatina in G Major, Op. 100
(Urtext)

FAURÉ, GABRIEL (1845 - 1924)
____ (K04345) Romance, Op. 28 (Urtext)
____ (K03484) Sonata in A Major, Op. 13

HANDEL, GEORGE FRIDERIC (1685 - 1759)
____ (K09798) Chamber Sonata No. 4, Op.
1-3 (Cello optional)
____ (K09207) Six Sonatas, Vol. I, Nos. 1-3
____ (K09208) Six Sonatas, Vol. II, Nos. 4-6

HAYDN, FRANZ JOSEPH (1732 - 1809)
____ (K09209) Violin Sonatas, Vol. I,
Nos. 1-4

KABALEVSKY, DMITRI (1904 - 1987)
____ (K03565) Violin Concerto

KREISLER, FRITZ (1875 - 1950)
____ (K09934) Romanze, Op. 4
____ (K09939) Tambourin Chinois

MENDELSSOHN, FELIX (1809 - 1847)
____ (K03668) Violin Concerto,
Op. 64 (Flesch)

MOZART, LEOPOLD (1719 - 1787)
____ (K04400) 12 Little Pieces from the
Notebook of Wolfgang
Mozart

MOZART, WOLFGANG AMADEUS (1756 - 1791)
____ (K03735) 20 Sonatas (Urtext)—
Vol. I: K. 57, 58, 60, 269,
301, 302, 303, 304, 305,
306, 376, 377
____ (K03736) 20 Sonatas (Urtext)—
Vol. II: K. 378, 379, 380,
402, 454, 481,
526, 547
____ (K04406) Violin Concerto No. 1,
K. 207
____ (K03737) Violin Concerto No. 3
in G Major, K. 216
____ (K03738) Violin Concerto No. 4,
K. 218

NARDINI, PIETRO (1722 - 1793)
____ (K09213) Sonata in D Major

PAGANINI, NICCOLO (1782 - 1840)
____ (K03765) Moto Perpetuo, Op. 11

PAGANINI—Kreisler
____ (K04359) Theme with Variations,
Op. 13 (J. Palpitti)

RACHMANINOFF, SERGEI (1873 - 1943)
____ (K04348) Hungarian Dance (Urtext)

SAINT-SAËNS CAMILLE (1835 - 1921)
____ (K04346) Danse Macabre, Op. 40
Transcribed by Composer

SAINT-SAËNS (YSAYE)
____ (K04369) Havanaise, Op. 83 (Urtext)

SCHUMANN, ROBERT (1810 - 1856)
____ (K04373) Sonata in A minor, Op. 105

SEITZ, FRIEDRICH (1848 - 1918)
____ (K03945) Student's Concerto No. I
in D (1st to 7th Pos.)
____ (K03947) Student's Concerto No. III
in G minor, Op.12 (1st
to 5th Pos.)
____ (K03948) Student's Concerto No. IV
in D (3rd Pos.)

SIBELIUS, JAN (1865 - 1957)
____ (K04690) Violin Concerto, Op. 47

SPOHR, LOUIS (1784 - 1859)
____ (K04377) Violin Concerto No. 8,
Op. 47

STRAUSS, RICHARD (1864 - 1949)
____ (K04353) Sonata in E-flat Major,
Op. 18

SUK, JOSEF (1874 - 1935)
____ (K04340) Four Pieces, Vol. I—
Op. 17 Nos. 1, 2

VITALI, TOMMASO (1665 - 1717)
____ (K04388) Chaconne in G minor

STRING INSTRUMENTS

Viola Alone

HOFMANN, R. (1844 - 1918)
____ (K04283)   First Studies, Op. 86

KAYSER, H.E. (1815 - 1888)
____ (K04284)   36 Studies, Op. 43

KREUTZER, R.R. (1766 - 1831)
____ (K04285)   42 Studies

PAGANINI, NICCOLO (1784 - 1840)
____ (K04293)   24 Caprices, Op. 1 (Transcribed
                 for Viola Solo)

SCHRADIECK, H. (1849 - 1918)
____ (K04289)   School of Viola Technique,
                 Vol. I

Viola and Piano

BEETHOVEN, LUDWIG van (1770 - 1827)
____ (K04309)   Two Romances, Op. 40,
                 50 (arranged)

BRAHMS, JOHANNES (1833 - 1897)
____ (K04310)   2 Sonatas, Op. 120
                 (Originally for Clarinet—
                 transcribed for Viola)

HANDEL, GEORGE FRIDERIC (1685 - 1759)
____ (K04312)   Sonata

HOFFMEISTER, F.A. (1754 - 1812)
____ (K04336)   Viola Concerto in D Major

JUON, PAUL (1872 - 1940)
____ (K04302)   Sonata in D Major, Op. 15

MARCELLO, BENEDETTO (1686 - 1739)
____ (K04313)   Sonata in E minor

MENDELSSOHN, FELIX (1809 - 1847)
____ (K04297)   Sonata

SCHUMANN, ROBERT (1810 - 1856)
____ (K04322)   Three Romances, Op. 94

STAMITZ, KARL (1747 - 1801)
____ (K04315)   Concerto in D Major,
                 Op. 1

VITALI, TOMMASO ANTONIO (1665 - 1717)
____ (K04316)   Chaconne in G minor

VIVALDI, ANTONIO (1678 - 1741)
____ (K04298)   Concerto for Viola
                 d'Amore (transcribed)

Viola Collections

ALBUM OF CLASSICAL PIECES (KLENGEL)
18th Century Composers
____ (K04303)   Vol. I
____ (K04304)   Vol. II
____ (K04305)   Vol. III

Cello Alone

BACH, JOHANN SEBASTIAN (1685 - 1750)
____ (K04412)   Six Suites for Cello Solo

DOTZAUER, J.J.F. (1783 - 1860)
____ (K04413)   113 Studies—Vol. I
                 Nos. 1-34
____ (K04416)   113 Studies—Vol. IV
                 Nos. 86-113

KABALEVSKY, DMITRI (1904 - 1987)
____ (K04422)   Five Studies in Major
                 and Minor

POPPER, DAVID (1843 - 1913)
____ (K04425)   High School of Cello
                 Playing, Op. 73
____ (K04426)   15 Etudes for Cello,
                 Op. 76

Cello and Piano

BACH, CARL PHILIPP EMANUEL (1714 - 1788)
____ (K09105)   Cello Concerto in A minor

BACH, JOHANN SEBASTIAN (1685 - 1750)
____ (K04428)   Three Sonatas for Viola
                 da Gamba, BWV 1027-29.
                 (Transcribed for Cello and
                 Piano by Julius Klengel)

BRAHMS, JOHANNES (1833 - 1897)
____ (K09110)   Sonata No. 1 in E minor,
                 Op. 38

FAURÉ, GABRIEL (1845 - 1924)
____ (K04431)   Sicilienne, Op. 78

GLAZUNOV, ALEXANDER (1865 - 1936)
____ (K09116)   Chant du Menstrel, Op. 71

GRIEG, EDVARD (1843 - 1907)
____ (K09117)   Elegiac Melodies, Op. 34

LALO, EDOUARD (1823 - 1892)
____ (K03606)   Concerto in D minor

MARCELLO, BENEDETTO (1686 - 1739)
____ (K09242)   Sonata in A minor
                 for Cello and Piano

VIVALDI, ANTONIO (1678 - 1741)
____ (K09129)   Six Sonatas for Cello
                 and B.C. — P

Cello Collections

MASTERS FOR THE YOUNG—HAYDN AND MOZART
____ (K09125)

String Bass Studies

SIMANDL, F. (1840 - 1912)
____ (K04451)   30 Etudes for Double Bass

String Bass and Piano

BACH, JOHANN SEBASTIAN (1685 -1750)
____ (EL03963)   Three Sonatas

BOTTESINI, GIOVANNI (1821 - 1889)
___ • (K04454)   Elegy

DRAGONETTI, DOMENICO (1763 - 1846)
____ (K04456)   Student's Concerto

GLIERE, REINHOLD (1875 - 1956)
____ (K04458)   Four Pieces.
____ (K09786)   Intermezzo, Op. 9, No. 1

KOUSSEVITZKY, SERGE (1874 - 1951)
____ (K04459)   Concerto, Op. 3

• = available as an authorized photocopy only

STRING ENSEMBLES

ENSEMBLES

NOTE: The following abbreviations are used throughout the listing of Duos, Trios and large ensembles:

B.C.—Basso Continuo
Sc—Complete Score and all parts, but no Piano
P—Complete Score and parts, with Keyboard or Piano Parts.

Titles without above abbreviations have only complete sets of parts.

Duos for Violin and Viola

GASTOLDI, GIOVANNI (1550 - 1622)
____ (K04655)   Six Duets

MOZART, WOLFGANG AMADEUS (1756 - 1791)
____ (K04657)   Twelve Duets, K. 487
                 (Arranged)
____ (K04658)   Two Duets, K. 423, K. 424

PLEYEL, IGNAZ (1757 - 1831)
____ (K04660)   Three Grand Duets, Op. 69

Duos for Violin and Cello

BEETHOVEN, LUDWIG van (1770 - 1827)
____ (K04694)   Three Duets for Violin and Cello

LASSO, ORLANDO di (1532 - 1733)
____ (K04703)   Six Fantasies

STAMITZ, KARL (1745 - 1801)
____ (K09725)   Six Duets, Op. 19

Duos for Viola and Cello

BEETHOVEN, LUDWIG van (1770 - 1827)
____ (K04695)   Duet for Viola and Cello

String Trios
Violin, Viola and Cello

BOCCHERINI, LUIGI (1743 - 1805)
____ (K03225)   Three Trios, Op. 38

HAYDN, FRANZ JOSEPH (1732 - 1809)
____ (K03538)   Three Divertimenti

MOZART, WOLFGANG AMADEUS (1756 - 1791)
____ (K03742)   Divertimento in E-flat Major, K. 563

SCHUBERT, FRANZ (1797 - 1828)
____ (K03871)   Trio No. 1 in B-flat Major
____ (K04780)   Trio No. 2 in B-flat Major

Collection

EASY FANTASIAS BY BASSANO, LUPO AND MORELY
____ (K04758)

Two Violins and Cello

HAYDN, FRANZ JOSEPH (1732 - 1809)
____ (K03539)   Twelve German Dances
                 (Arranged)—Sc

MOZART, WOLFGANG AMADEUS (1756 - 1791)
____ (K03743)   Five Viennese Serenades K. 439b

PACHELBEL, JOHANN (1653 - 1706)
____ (K04776)   Two Trio Suites (C Major, B-flat Major) B.C.—P

VIVALDI, ANTONIO (1678 - 1741)
____ (K04786)   Sonatas da Camera a Tre, Op. 1, Vol. I, Nos. 1-6 — P.

Other String Trios

ROSSI, SALOMONE (1570 - c. 1630)
____ (K04778)   Sonata in D minor for Two Violins and Chitarrone (or Cello) — P.

VITALI, TOMMASO ANTONIO (1665 - 1717)
____ (K09618)   Sonata for Violin, Cello and Harpsichord (Op. 4, No. 11) — Sc

Collections

EASY PIECES FOR THREE VIOLINS
(VARIOUS GERMAN COMPOSERS)
____ (K04756)   Vol. I

EASY FANTASIAS FOR THREE VIOLAS
____ (K04758)   Works by Bassano, Lupo and Morley—Sc

Piano Trios
Violin, Cello and Piano

ARENSKY, ANTON (1861 - 1906)
____ (K03010)   Trio in D minor, Op. 32

BEETHOVEN, LUDWIG van (1770 - 1827)
____ (K09707)   Piano Trio No. 1 - Op. 1, No. 1
____ (K09708)   Piano Trio No. 2 - Op. 1, No. 2
____ (K09709)   Piano Trio No. 3 - Op. 1, No. 3
____ (K09712)   Piano Trio No. 6 - Op. 70, No. 2
____ (K09713)   Piano Trio No. 7 - Op. 97

BRAHMS, JOHANNES (1833 - 1897)
____ (K09604)   Trio in C Major, Op. 87

CHOPIN, FREDERIC (1810 - 1849)
____ (K09628)   Piano Trio in G minor, Op. 8

HAYDN, FRANZ JOSEPH (1732 - 1809)
____ (K09613)   Trios for Violin, Cello & Piano Vol. I (Nos. 1-6)
____ (K09614)   Trios for Violin, Cello & Piano Vol. II (Nos. 7-12)
____ (K09615)   Trios for Violin, Cello & Piano Vol. III (Nos. 13-17)

MENDELSSOHN, FELIX (1809 - 1847)
____ (K09635)   Trio in D minor, Op. 49
____ (K09636)   Trio in C minor, Op. 66

MOZART, WOLFGANG AMADEUS (1756 - 1791)
____ (K09631)   Trio No. 1 in G Major, K. 49

RACHMANINOFF, SERGEI (1873 - 1943)
____ (K09605)   Trio Elegiaque, Op. 9

RUBINSTEIN, ANTON (1830 - 1894)
____ (K09623)   Trio No. 2 in G Major (Op. 15, No. 2)

SAINT-SAËNS, CAMILLE (1835 - 1921)
____ (K09621)   Trio, Op. 18
____ (K09637)   Trio No. 2, Op. 92

SCHUBERT, FRANZ (1797 - 1828)
____ (K09622)   Trio No. 1 in B-flat Major, Op. 99
____ (K09619)   Trio No. 2 in E-flat Major, Op. 100

SCHUMANN, ROBERT (1810 - 1856)
____ (K09633)   Trio No. 1, Op. 53

SMETANA, BEDRICH (1824 - 1884)
____ (K09629)   Trio in G minor, Op. 15

TSCHAIKOWSKY, PETER ILYICH (1840 - 1893)
____ (K09611)   Trio in A minor, Op. 50

VITALI, TOMMASO ANTONIO (1665 - 1717)
____ (K09618)   Sonata in B minor (Op. 4, No. 11).

STRING INSTRUMENTS

String Quartets

BEETHOVEN, LUDWIG van (1770 - 1827)
Revised by Joachim and Moser
____ (K03143)   String Quartets Vol. I,
             Op. 18, Nos. 1-6
____ (K03144)   String Quartets Vol. II,
             Op. 59, Nos. 1-3;
             Op. 74; Op. 95
____ (K03145)   String Quartets Vol. III,
             Op. 127, 130, 131,132,
             133, 135.

BOCCHERINI, LUIGI (1743 - 1805)
____ (K03226)   Nine Selected String Quartets.

BRAHMS, JOHANNES (1833 - 1897)
____ (K03240)   Three String Quartets, Op. 51,
             Nos. 1 & 2, Op. 67

CHOPIN, FREDERIC (1810 - 1849)
____ (K09679)   Etude (Op. 25, No. 7)
             (arr. by M. Balakirew)

DVORAK, ANTONIN, (1841 - 1904)
____ (K09678)   Quartet in F minor, Op. 9
____ (K03424)   String Quartet in F, Op. 96

GRIEG, EDVARD (1843 - 1907)
____ (K03488)   String Quartet, Op. 27

HAYDN, FRANZ JOSEPH (1732 - 1809)
Revised by Andreas Moser and Hugo Dechert
____ (K03543)   30 Celebrated String Quartets,
             Vol. I - Op. 9, No. 2;
             Op. 17, No. 5; Op. 50,
             No. 6; Op. 54, Nos. 1,
             2, 3; Op. 64, Nos. 2,
             3, 4; Op. 74, Nos. 1,
             2, 3; Op. 77, Nos. 1, 2
____ (K03544)   30 Celebrated String Quartets,
             Vol. II - Op. 3, Nos. 3, 5;
             Op. 20, Nos. 4, 5, 6; Op. 33,
             Nos. 2, 3, 6; Op. 64,
             Nos. 5, 6; Op. 76, Nos. 1,
             2, 3, 4, 5, 6

MENDELSSOHN, FELIX (1809 - 1847)
____ (K03669)   String Quartets, Op. 12;
             Op. 44, Nos. 1, 2 & 3

**MOZART, WOLFGANG AMADEUS
(1756 - 1791)**
____ (K03747)   Divertimenti, K. 136, 137, 138
____ (K03745)   16 Easy String Quartets, K. 155,
             156, 157, 158, 159, 160, 168,
             169, 170, 171,172, 173, 285,
             298, 370, 546
____ (K03744)   Ten Famous Quartets - Revised
             by Andreas Moser and Hugo
             Becker, K. 387, 421, 428,
             458, 464, 465, 499, 575,
             589, 590

RAVEL, MAURICE (1875 - 1937)
____ (K03840)   String Quartet in F Major

**RIMSKY-KORSAKOV, NICOLAI
(1844 - 1908)**
____ (K05248)   Three String Quartets: Variations
             No. 4 in G Major from
             "Variations on a Russian
             Theme" by various composers;
             Allegro in B-flat Major from
             the Album "Fridays" by
             various composers; Four
             Variations on a Chorale

SCHUBERT, FRANZ (1797 - 1828)
____ (K03874)   String Quartets, edited
             by Ferdinand David and
             revised by Carl Herrmann
             Vol. I: Op. 29; Op. 125,
             Nos. 1 & 2; Op. Posth.
             in D minor
____ (K03875)   String Quartets, edited
             by Ferdinand David and
             revised by Carl Herrmann
             Vol. II: Op. 161; Op. 168;
             Op. Posth. in G minor,
             D Major, F minor

SCHUMANN, ROBERT (1810 - 1856)
____ (K03932)   String Quartets, Op. 41,
             Nos. 1, 2 & 3.

SIBELIUS, JAN (1865 - 1957)
____ (K03978)   Voces Intimae, Op. 56
             (in D minor)

TSCHAIKOWSKY, PETER ILYICH (1840 - 1893)
____ (K04014)   String Quartet in D
             Major, Op. 11.

WOLF, HUGO (1860 - 1903)
____ (K04044)   Italian Serenade.

String Quartet Collections

ALBUM OF EASY STRING QUARTETS
Pieces by Bach, Haydn, Mozart, Beethoven,
Schumann, Mendelssohn and others.
____ (K03425)   Vol. I
____ (K03426)   Vol. II
____ (K03427)   Vol. III

Piano Quartets with Strings

BRAHMS, JOHANNES (1833 - 1897)
____ (K09645)   Piano Quartet No. 1
             in G minor, Op. 25
____ (K09647)   Piano Quartet No. 3
             in C minor, Op. 60

DVORAK, ANTONIN (1841 - 1904)
____ (K09642)   Quartet in E-flat Major,
             Op. 87

FAURÉ, GABRIEL (1845 - 1904)
____ (K09640)   Quartet No. 2 in G minor,
             Op. 45

MENDELSSOHN, FELIX (1809 - 1847)
____ (K09718)   Piano Quartet, Op. 1

MOZART, WOLFGANG AMADEUS (1756 - 1791)
____ (K09649)   Quartet in E-flat Major,
             K. 493

SCHUMANN, ROBERT (1810 - 1856)
____ (K09641)   Quartet in E-flat Major,
             Op. 47

String Quintets

BOCCHERINI, LUIGI (1743 - 1805)
____ (K09450)   Third Quintet in E minor
             (for Two Violins, Viola,
             Cello and Guitar)

DVORAK, ANTONIN (1841 - 1904)
____ (K09676)   Quintet in G Major,
             Op. 77

MENDELSSOHN, FELIX (1809 - 1847)
____ (K09675)   Quintets, Op. 18 (A Major)
             & Op. 87 (B Major)

MOZART, WOLFGANG AMADEUS (1756 - 1791)
____ (K03746)   Eine Kleine Nachtmusik,
             K. 525
____ (K03748)   String Quintets (Two
             Violins, Two Violas,
             Cello) K. 406, 515,
             516, 593, 614.

SCHUBERT, FRANZ (1797 - 1828)
____ (K03872)   String Quintet in C Major, Op. 163
             (Two Violins, Viola,
             Two Cellos)

Piano Quintets with Strings

BORODIN, ALEXANDER (1833 - 1887)
____ (K09658)   Quintet in C minor

BRAHMS, JOHANNES (1833 - 1897)
____ (K09651)   Piano Quintet in F minor,
             Op. 34

SCHUBERT, FRANZ (1797 - 1828)
____ (K03873)   Trout Quintet, for Piano,
             Violin, Viola, Cello
             and Bass, Op. 114

SCHUMANN, ROBERT (1810 - 1856)
____ (K09652)   Quintet, Op. 44

String Sextets and Octets

BRAHMS, JOHANNES (1833 - 1897)
____ (K03252)   Sextet in B-flat Major, Op. 18
             (Two Violins, Two Violas,
             Two Cellos)

MENDELSSOHN, FELIX (1809 - 1847)
____ (K03675)   String Octet in E-flat Major,
             Op. 20 (Four Violins, Two
             Violas, Two Cellos)

SCHOENBERG, ARNOLD (1874 - 1951)
____ (K09699)   Verklaerte Nacht (Two
             Violins, Two Violas,
             Two Cellos)

Harp Music

KASTNER, ALFRED (1870 - 1948)
____ (K04686)   Ten Etudes, Op. 2